WHO'S AFRAID
OF THE *Quite Nice* WOLF?

D1147142

For Lucas, Sammy and Daisy,
my very own (nice) Wolf Pack
~ K B

To my best intentions
~ L W

First published in the UK in 2019
This edition published 2019
by New Frontier Publishing Europe Ltd
Uncommon, 126 New King's Rd, Fulham, London SW6 4LZ
www.newfrontierpublishing.co.uk

ISBN: 978-1-912858-36-1

A CIP catalogue record for this book
is available from the British Library.

Designed by Verity Clark

Printed in China · 10 9 8 7 6 5 4 3 2

WHO'S AFRAID
OF THE Quite Nice WOLF?

KITTY BLACK

LAURA WOOD

NEW FRONTIER PUBLISHING

'Anyone for tea?'

Wilfred was a wolf.

But not a scary one.

He lived in a pack.
But not a nice one.

best WOOL in
THE world

WANTED

10.000

10.000

10.0

'Oh gosh!
Oh no!'

'Eeeek!'

Wilfred tried his best to fit in.

'Maybe you'd like to be eaten?'

It never worked out.

'Cheerio!'

'I'll be back to help you with the carrots next week!'

No-one was afraid of the Quite Nice Wolf. (For a wolf, he was quite nice.)

'Wilfred!' growled the Leader of the Wolf Pack. 'A wolf is fearsome, bold and scary!'

'Like this? **Grr!**'

'Ack!' 'Cough!'

'I do apologise.'

'You are quiet, you're helpful, and you're even . . . **A VEGETARIAN!**'

'Everyone needs their greens,' Wilfred pleaded.

'Who's afraid of the *Quite Nice Wolf*?'
asked the Leader.

'No-one!'

cried the Pack.

'Oh dear,'
sighed Wilfred.

'Tomorrow,' said the Leader, 'we attack the sheep.'

'What, all of them?' asked Wilfred.

'You will learn to be a proper wolf! You will join us!'

'ME?!'

The Wolf Pack howled all night.

'Arooooo!'

Wilfred tried to sleep. Another hot water bottle, perhaps?

Snip! Snip!

I could run away! he thought. I could start a new life as a hair stylist!

I could become a vet for baby chickens!

Or even write poetry for the Queen!

'Er-herm!'

'Oooo!'

Thinking about attacking the sheep gave him a tummy ache.

I have to help them! thought Wilfred, and off he went with his thermos.

'Wilfred!' said Mildred. 'It's not Poker Thursday.'
'It's an emergency!' said Wilfred.
'Tomorrow night, there will be – a Wolf Pack Attack!'

'Cocoa?'

'Oh no!' cried Mildred. 'We'll all be eaten! We have to run away!'
'What if there was another way?' asked Wilfred.
Together they came up with a plan.

Training commenced first thing the next morning.
'Welcome to being a Big Bad Sheep,' said Mildred.

'Sheep are fearsome.'
'FEARSOME!'

'Sheep are bold.'
'BOLD!'

'Sheep are scary.'
'SCARY!'

'Baaa!'

'Who's white,
fluffy and lethal?'
'WE ARE!'

'For me?'

Mildred gave Wilfred a
special present. 'It's perfect!'
said Wilfred.

The next day the Wolf Pack hunted.

'Arooooo!
We're coming for
youuuuu!'

But wait.

What is this?

Sheep are small,
tasty and **terrified** . . .

. . . aren't they?

Wilfred threw on his special present.
The wool was lovely and soft.

'NOW!' he shouted.

'Wilfred!' he cried. 'You did this?
You are not a proper wolf!'

'You're right,' said Wilfred,
'I am not a proper wolf.
No-one is afraid of the Quite
Nice Wolf, but I like being nice,
and I think I'll live here now.'

'GRR,'
growled the Leader.

'Ahem?'

'Fine, fine,' said the
Leader, slinking away.

'We're out of here!'

No-one was afraid of the Big Bad Wolf anymore.
But the wolves were afraid of the Big Bad Sheep.

And Wilfred the Quite Nice Wolf? He planted sunflowers.

'Time for tea, Wilfred!'